USING THIS BOOK

*Children learn to read by **reading**, but they need help to begin.*

When you have read the story on the left-hand pages aloud to the child, go back to the beginning of the book and look at the pictures together.

Encourage children to read the sentences under the pictures. If they don't know a word, give them a chance to "guess" what it is from the illustrations before telling them.

There are more suggestions for helping children learn to read in the *Parent/Teacher Guide*.

LADYBIRD BOOKS, INC.
Lewiston, Maine 04240 U.S.A.
© Text and layout SHEILA McCULLAGH MCMLXXXVI
© In publication LADYBIRD BOOKS LTD MCMLXXXVI
Loughborough, Leicestershire, England

Printed in England

Never Trust Dragons

written by SHEILA McCULLAGH
illustrated by JON DAVIS

This book belongs to:

_____

Ladybird Books

Tessa was a little cat
who lived in Puddle Lane.
One sunny day, Tessa went
to see the Magician,
who lived in the big house
at the end of the lane.
She climbed up the tree,
and jumped down onto the roof.
She ran up the roof to the skylight,
and looked down into
the Magician's room.

Tessa looked down.

The Magician wasn't there.
At first, Tessa thought
the room was empty.
But then she saw
a little puff of smoke
coming out of the cage
on the table.
"The dragon is there,"
she said to herself.
"But he's safe in his cage.
I'll go and see him."

"I will go and see the
dragon," said Tessa.

Tessa climbed down the pole
that was propped against the wall.
She ran across to the table,
and jumped up onto it.
There was the dragon's cage.
The dragon was lying inside it.
His eyes were shut.
He was fast asleep.
He was breathing out puffs of smoke.

The little dragon
was fast asleep.

Tessa went one step closer.

The dragon woke up.

He opened one eye, and

looked at her.

Tessa jumped back.

The little dragon lifted his head.

"Don't be afraid of me," he said.

"I wouldn't hurt **you**.

The Magician put me in here

because I wanted to eat a mouse.

There's nothing wrong with eating mice,

is there?"

The dragon woke up.
He opened one eye.
He saw Tessa.

"N-no," said Tessa. "But
you mustn't eat the mice
who live in the garden.
We've all promised not to do that."
"I've promised, too," said the dragon.
"But the Magician still
won't let me out!
And I'm **so** stiff!
Do you think you could
open the latch on the door,
so that I could come out
and fly around the room just once?
I'd fly straight back to the cage,
and you could shut the door again.
Please let me out!"

"Let me out!"
said the little dragon.

The little dragon looked so miserable,
that Tessa felt sorry for him.
"Do you **promise** to fly
straight back to the cage?"
she asked.

"Of course I do," said the dragon.

"Then I'll let you out for
just one minute," said Tessa.
She jumped on top of the cage.
She pressed the latch,
and let the dragon out.

Tessa let the dragon out.

The dragon flew up into the air.
He breathed out fire, and
he breathed out smoke.
He swung around,
and flew straight at Tessa,
breathing out smoke and fire.
Tessa didn't wait to talk
about promises.
She leaped right off the table
into an empty box
that was standing on the floor,
and she pulled down the lid
with a bang!

The dragon flew out.
He flew at Tessa.
Tessa jumped into a box.

The dragon flew down onto the box.
He was just about to pull up the lid,
when he heard the Magician coming.
The Magician came in.

The Magician came in.

The dragon flew out
the open window.
The Magician ran across the room.
"Come back!" he shouted.
"Come back!"
But the dragon flew on.
Tessa heard the Magician calling.
She looked out of the box.
"Meow!" said Tessa.
She was very frightened.

The dragon flew out
the open window.
Tessa looked out of the box.

The Magician turned around,
and saw her.

"Oh, Tessa!" he said.

"What **have** you been doing?"

"I let the dragon out," said Tessa.

"And I'm very sorry.
But he **promised** to fly back
into his cage again."

"**Never** trust dragons,"
said the Magician.

"Dragons never keep their promises."

"Never trust dragons,"
said the Magician.

The little dragon flew down
onto the garden wall.
He saw Mr. Gotobed
sitting in the lane.
Mr. Gotobed was fast asleep,
with a newspaper over his face.
The dragon flew down.
He breathed out fire, and
he breathed out smoke.
Mr. Gotobed's newspaper
began to burn.

The little dragon
saw Mr. Gotobed.
Mr. Gotobed was fast asleep.

Mr. Gotobed woke up in a fright.
He saw the newspaper burning.
He threw down the newspaper,
and jumped to his feet.

He stamped out the fire.

The little dragon flew away,
down Puddle Lane.

Mr. Gotobed didn't see him.
He went into his house, and
made himself a cup of tea.
Then he went to bed,
to recover from the shock.

Mr. Gotobed woke up.

The little dragon flew over the rooftops.
He looked down, and saw Pedro and Davy.
Pedro and Davy were in Davy's yard.
They had a big tin tub,
full of water, and they were
sailing paper boats in it.

The little dragon flew down
like an arrow.
He breathed out fire, and
he breathed out smoke.
All the paper boats
went up in flames.

The little dragon
saw Pedro and Davy.
He flew down.

Pedro picked up a bucket of water.
He threw it over the dragon.
The water turned into
a cloud of steam,
and the dragon was **very** wet.

The dragon was very wet.

The dragon was very angry, too.
He shook off the water, and
flew back over the rooftop,
and down into Puddle Lane.
"I'll burn a house down!"
he said to himself.
"I'll burn a house down,
if it takes me all day!"
The dragon looked across Puddle Lane,
and he saw Mr. Puffle.
Mr. Puffle was watering his flowers.

The dragon looked down
Puddle Lane.
He saw Mr. Puffle.

The dragon flew down
to Mr. Puffle's front door.
He breathed out fire, and
he breathed out smoke.
The door began to burn.
Mr. Puffle looked down.
He saw the dragon.
He picked up a flowerpot
and dropped it on the dragon's head!

Mr. Puffle looked down.
He saw the dragon.

The flowerpot hit the little dragon
so hard, that it knocked him out.
Mr. Puffle went downstairs.
He found the dragon lying in the lane,
and he picked him up.
"I'll tie you up, before you have a chance
to do any more damage,"
said Mr. Puffle. "You can light
my fire for me every day,
and save me a lot of trouble."
The little dragon didn't say anything.
He didn't hear Mr. Puffle.
He was still knocked out.

Mr. Puffle picked up the dragon.

Mr. Puffle took the little dragon
into his back yard.
He put a dog collar around
the dragon's neck, and
he fixed a chain to it.
When the little dragon
opened his eyes,
he found himself chained up.

The little dragon
opened his eyes.

So the little dragon lived
at Mr. Puffle's house.
Mr. Puffle kept him chained up
in the yard all day.
But every morning he took him inside,
to light the fire.

So the little dragon was very useful
to Mr. Puffle, and he had to stay
in Mr. Puffle's yard
for a **very** long time.

The little dragon
lit Mr. Puffle's fire for him.

Look at the pictures.

What is happening in this picture?

What has happened in this picture?

What do you think happened next?

Notes for the parent/teacher

Turn back to the beginning, and print the child's name in the space on the title page, using ordinary, not capital letters.

Now go through the book again. Look at each picture and talk about it. Point to the caption and read it aloud.

Run your finger under the words as you read, so that the child learns that reading goes from left to right.

Encourage the child to read the words under the illustrations. Don't rush in with the word before he/she has had time to think, but don't leave him/her struggling.

Read this story as often as the child likes hearing it. The more opportunities he/she has to look at the illustrations and **read** the captions with you, the sooner he/she will come to recognize the words.

If you have several books, let the child choose which story he/she would like.

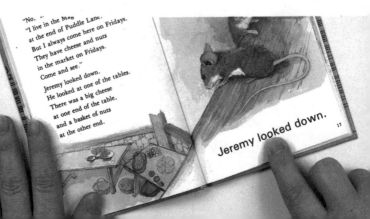

"No. "
"I live in the Mop at the end of Puddle Lane.
But I always come here on Fridays.
They have cheese and nuts in the market on Fridays.
Come and see."

Jeremy looked down.
He looked at one of the tables.
There was a big cheese at one end of the table, and a basket of nuts at the other end.

Jeremy looked down.

17